THE SILLY TAIL BOOK

A Parents Magazine
READ ALOUD Original.

THE SILLY TAIL BOOK

Marc Brown

Parents Magazine Press • New York

For Katherine
and Jonathan Walmsey

Library of Congress Cataloging in Publication Data
Brown, Marc.
The silly tail book.
Summary: A short poem describing what tails are
and aren't, what they can do and can't, where they
grow and don't.
[1. Tails—Fiction.   2. Stories in rhyme]   I.   Title.
PZ8.3.B8147Si   1983   [E]   83-2250
ISBN 0-8193-1109-X

If you grow a tail,
you grow only one.

But growing more tails
could be much more fun!

Tails go fast
and tails go slow.

A tail will follow
wherever you go.

Tails grow on all kinds
of creatures.
Tails have all kinds
of features.

Think of the things
a tail can do.
Swing from trees,

or shine a shoe.

Kangaroos use them
to jump up high.

Cows use them
to swat a fly.

There are tails for riding

and tails for hiding...

Tails with bows

walking in rows.

A kite tail can be red or blue.
Maybe you have a tail or two.

Some tails are curly,

some straight with spots.

Some tails are striped,

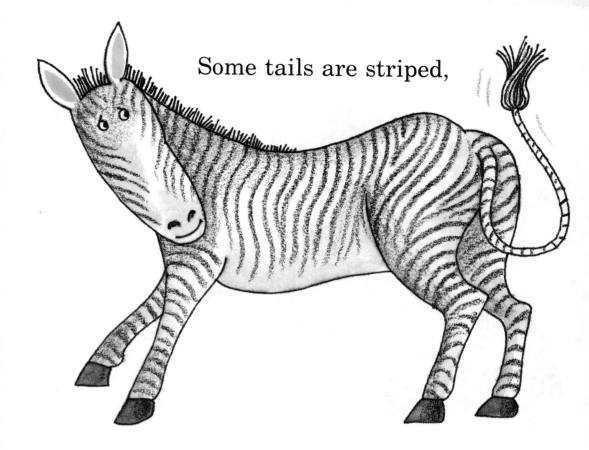

others are not.

Happy tails wag.

Sad tails drag.

Look for tails on the loud,
and tails on the proud.

For seal tails flipping
and whale tails flopping...

One hundred rabbits
with cotton tails hopping.

There were tails long ago
with spikes and bumps.

There are tails today
found behind two humps.

A tail would look silly
up front for a nose.

It belongs at the end
and that's where it goes.

About the author/artist

MARC BROWN is the author/illustrator
of many children's books including, for
Parents, WITCHES FOUR and PICKLE
THINGS. Mr. Brown travels frequently
around the country visiting schools and
says he gets many story ideas during
such visits. He also tries out new story
ideas on his two sons. Mr. Brown lives
in an old house by the sea in Hingham,
Massachusetts.